ANIMAL ANTICS **A** TO **Z**®

Nina Nandu's Nervous Noggin

by Barbara deRubertis • illustrated by R.W. Alley

THE KANE PRESS / NEW YORK

Alpha Betty's Class

Alexander Anteater

Bobby Baboon

Corky Cub

Dily Dog

Eddie Elephant

Frances Frog

Gertie Gorilla

Hanna Hippo

Lena Llama

Izzy Impala

Jeremy Jackrabbit

Kylie Kangaroo

Maxwell Moose

Library of Congress Cataloging-in-Publication Data

deRubertis, Barbara.
Nina Nandu's nervous noggin / by Barbara deRubertis ; illustrated by R.W. Alley.
p. cm. — (Animal antics A to Z)
Summary: Nina Nandu has just moved to a new neighborhood and she does not want to go to a new school, but
once she is welcomed by the other students she feels much less nervous.
ISBN 978-1-57565-335-8 (library binding : alk. paper) — ISBN 978-1-57565-326-6 (pbk. : alk. paper)
[1. Birds—Fiction. 2. First day of school—Fiction. 3. Schools—Fiction. 4. Moving, Household—Fiction.
5. Animals—Fiction. 6. Alphabet.] I. Alley, R. W. (Robert W.), ill. II. Title.
PZ7.D4475Ni 2011
[E]—dc22   2010021825

1 3 5 7 9 10 8 6 4 2

First published in the United States of America in 2011 by Kane Press, Inc.
Printed in the United States of America
WOZ0111

Series Editor: Juliana Hanford
Book Design: Edward Miller

Animal Antics A to Z is a registered trademark of Kane Press, Inc.

www.kanepress.com

Nina Nandu had just moved to a new neighborhood.
But Nina did NOT want to go to a new school.

She was nervous about meeting new kids.
She was nervous about having a new teacher.

Granny Nandu brought Nina some hot cinnamon tea.

"Nina," said Granny. "You must turn off the nervous button in your noggin."

"What's my *noggin*?" asked Nina.

Granny gently knocked on Nina's head.
"*This* is your noggin. Now turn off that
nervous button in there!"

"I can't," said Nina.
"So I'm not going to school.
Nope. No way.
Not now. Not ever. Never!
I'm just too nervous in my noggin."

"Nonsense," said Granny Nandu.
"I went to your new school to meet your teacher, Alpha Betty.

You will be the only nandu in your class. One of a kind! Special!"

Nina frowned.
"I don't want to be the only nandu.
Nobody will know anything about nandus.

They'll think I'm an ostrich. Or an emu.
They'll make fun of me and call me names."

"So I'm not going to school," Nina announced.
"Nope. No way.
Not now. Not ever. Never!
I'm *waaay* too nervous in my noggin."

"Nonsense!" said Granny.

That night, Nina had a nightmare about school.

She dreamed that the children called her
"Nervous Nina Emu."

The next morning, the sun was shining.
But Nina Nandu was not.

"You'll need to leave for school soon,"
said Granny.

Nina frowned. "I'm not going to school.
Nope. No way.
Not now. Not ever. Never!
I'm MUCH too nervous in my noggin."

"Nonsense," said Granny.
She gave Nina a gentle nudge.

Nina wobbled down the narrow lane.

Her knees were knocking.
Her wings were numb.

Suddenly, Nina stumbled on a stone.

She landed on her nose and knees.

"*OUCH!*"

Granny called, "Are you okay, Nina?"

Nina cried, "I bumped my nose.
I banged my knees. And now my
noggin is even MORE nervous!"

Granny grabbed her nurse kit and ran to Nina.
She kissed Nina's nose. And she put nine
bandages on Nina's knees.

"Now do you feel better?" Granny asked.

Nina wailed. "I do NOT want to go to school.
Nope. No way.
Not now. Not ever. Never!
I'm just too NERVOUS in my noggin!"

"Nonsense," said Granny.
"I'll walk to school with you."

So Nina and Granny Nandu went
down the lane together.

Soon they arrived at Alpha Betty's school.

Granny said, "You'll be fine, Nina.
I'll meet you here after school."

Nina turned the knob on the door.

Her knees were knocking.
Her wings were numb.
Her noggin was very, very, VERY nervous.

But she went inside.

Alpha Betty and all the students cheered.

"Welcome, Nina!
We know you're not an ostrich!
We know you're not an emu!
You're a NANDU! And nandus are COOL!"

Hanna Hippo said, "Come sit next to me!"

Nina smiled.

Bobby Baboon asked, "Would you like a snack?
I brought some bananas to nibble on!"

"Thank you!" said Nina.

Soon Nina was making friends and having fun.
She listened to Eddie Elephant read his new story.

She ran a race with
Rosie Raccoon.

And she painted pictures
with Polly Porcupine.

Nina hardly noticed when the
bell rang at the end of the day.

Granny was waiting for Nina outside.
Nina ran over to her, smiling happily.

"Alpha Betty is nice! The kids are nice!
This school is FUN," said Nina Nandu.

"You mean, you weren't nervous?"
asked Granny.

"Nope." Nina grinned. "No way.
Not now. Not ever. Never!
My noggin won't be nervous ANYMORE!"

FUN FACTS

- Home: Nandus are native to South America.
- Family: *Nandu* is the Spanish name of the rhea. It is a member of the **ratite** family of large birds that cannot fly, which also includes the ostrich (Africa) and the emu (Australia).
- Appearance: Nandus have long legs for fast running. While running, they also spread out their wings which act like sails and help them run even faster!
- Size: Nandus can grow to be almost 5 feet tall and weigh close to 90 pounds.
- **Did You Know?** The mother nandu lays the eggs, but the father sits on the nest and keeps them warm. After the eggs hatch, the father will charge at anyone who comes near the little chicks!

LOOK BACK

Learning to identify letter sounds (phonemes) at the beginning, middle, and end of words is called "phonemic awareness."

- The word *nervous* <u>begins</u> with the *n* sound. Listen to the words on page 8 being read again. When you hear a word that begins with the *n* sound, gently knock on your noggin and say "Nnnnn!"
- The word *Nina* has the *n* sound at the <u>beginning</u> AND in the <u>middle</u>. Listen to the words on page 14 being read again. When you hear words that have the *n* sound in the <u>middle</u>, gently knock on your knee and say "Nnnnn!"
- **Challenge:** The word *can* <u>ends</u> with the *n* sound. What word do you have if you change the *c* to *f*? To *m*? To *p*? To *r*? To *v*?

TRY THIS!

Nnn, Nnn, Where Is the *Nnn* Sound?

- Write a large *n* on a piece of paper. Now sit on a chair and listen carefully as each word in the word bank is read aloud slowly.
- If the word <u>begins</u> with the *n* sound, hold the *n* above your head!
- If the word has the *n* sound in the <u>middle</u>, hold the *n* in front of your tummy!
- If the word <u>ends</u> with the *n* sound, hold the *n* above your feet!

noggin	pan	Granny	nervous
snack	raccoon	nurse	lane	grinned
button	shining	nose	

FOR MORE ACTIVITIES, go to Nina Nandu's website: www.kanepress.com/AnimalAntics/NinaNandu.htm
You'll also find a recipe for Nina Nandu's Chicken 'n' Noodles!